Billie Goes Back to School
Social Distancing for Children

Authored by Tara Travieso
Illustrated by Bazma Ahmad

ISBN: 978-1-7352808-4-4 (hardback), 978-1-7352808-5-1 (paperback) and 978-1-7352808-6-8 (ebook)

This book is dedicated to all of the children of the world.

May you enjoy your bubble, and remember that bubbles do not separate us from

LOVE,
kindness,
and
fun.

"Hi Mom!" Billie said as she got into her car.

"I had such a great day."

"Hi Honey Bunches. That's wonderful to hear.

Please tell me all about it."

"Ok. So, I saw so many friends. Paige, Tristan, and Shane are all in my class. Everyone looks older and bigger now."

Billie's mom smiled. "Of course they do, and so do you! You all grow so quickly, especially when you eat healthy foods like you do, Sweetie. Speaking of eating, did you like your lunch today?"

"Mom," Billie said in a serious voice. "I didn't just like my lunch, I loved my lunch!"

Billie and her mom looked at each other and burst into laugher.

When they were almost home, Billie saw two of her friends that lived nearby. "Mom, look, it's Brenden and Madison," she said as she waved hello to the children. "May I please go say hello and see how their first day went?" she asked her mother. "Sure, Honey, but just for a few minutes."

As soon as they arrived, Billie got out of the car and ran to her friends. "So, how was your first day of school?" Billie asked Brenden and Madison.

"Great! I wasn't sure what it was going to be like," Madison said.

This year, Madison was going to school virtually. "It's very different, but I really like it.

We all have cameras in our computers to see each other.

It's pretty neat."

"How do you raise a quiet hand when you want to talk?" asked Billie.

"There is a button you click with your mouse and then the teacher can call on you to speak. We all get to say hello and take turns reading, speaking, and asking questions throughout the day."

Madison continued, "Now that I don't have to take the school bus, I have more time to spend with my family. My dad and I even had enough time to make banana pancakes and eggs this morning."

"Banana pancakes! Mmmmm," Brenden said while rubbing his belly. "Those are my favorite."

"My teacher told us that we are going to go on virtual field trips."

"What does that mean, Madison?" Brenden asked.

"It means that we can visit places through our computer. We can take tours of famous art museums and see inside historic palaces all around the world!"

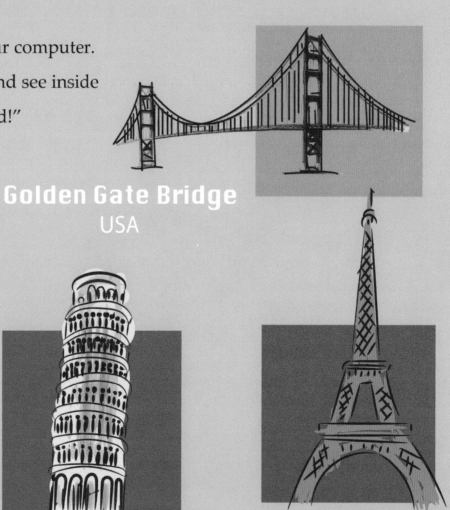

Golden Gate Bridge
USA

Big Ben
United Kingdom

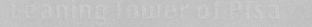
Leaning Tower of Pisa
Italy

Eiffel Tower
France

"Wow! I love to travel. That sounds incredible." Billie said, with a dreamy look in her eyes.

Machu Picchu
Peru

Statue of Liberty
USA

Taj Mahal
India

Pyramids of Giza
Egypt

"How was your day, Billie?" asked Madison.

"Well, I was really excited to get dressed
and meet my new classmates.
We have two new kids, Matthew and Marie,
that just moved to town.
They were a little shy at first."

"I told them all about our imaginary bubbles and
how they keep us clean, safe, and germ-free.
When I said they could also have an imaginary bubble,
they wanted a bubble right away! Then, they weren't shy anymore."

"We have some new rules to keep us safe and healthy."

Billie started to tell her friends about the new school policies.

There was a lot for her to learn.

If we have a fever,
we should stay home.

We should try not to
touch our face,
eyes, or mouth.

Everyone will be wearing a mask, and
the mask should cover the nose and mouth.

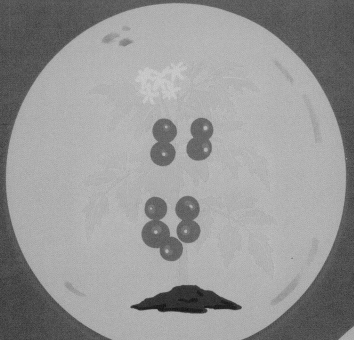

We will be outside more often doing things like gardening, playing sports, and other activities in the fresh air.

We can't drink from the water fountain.

We will wash our hands often.

"I picked out a new mask for school. It's pink with yellow polka dots!

Rob's mask has animals all over it. Michelle's has purple hearts, because purple is her favorite color.

There are eight students in our class this year, which means we have a smaller class than last year.

We all wear masks to school each day."

"My teacher is Mr. Edwards. He is really smart, and funny, too! He made our whole class laugh all day. Mr. Edwards even wore a mask with smiley faces on it!"

"How was your day, Brenden?" Madison asked.

Brenden was home-schooling this year.

"I woke up bright and early, excited for the first day,"
Brenden said. "Last night, I couldn't even go to sleep
I was so excited. My mom bought new books,
games, and art supplies. I couldn't wait to use them!"

Brenden's mom was teaching him lessons instead of a teacher. Brenden would do his work in his home with his little brother.

"Guess you will never forget your lunch at home again, right?" Billie joked.

"Good point, Billie. There's always something in the refrigerator!" Brenden laughed.

Brenden smiled and said happily, "Mom said we will go on field trips with some other kids that are being home-schooled. Next week, we're going to meet some friends at the beach for playtime."

Brenden continued, "Today, we went on a scavenger hunt in the neighborhood. We found all kinds of plants and insects. It was an interesting way to learn about the earth."

Madison chimed in, "We also went on a scavenger hunt, of sorts. Each of us had to go outside and collect something that was our favorite color. Then, we showed it to our classmates on the computer. Guess what I chose?"

Brenden and Billie looked at each other and shrugged their shoulders. "Your favorite color is yellow, so maybe a flower?" Brenden guessed. Billie guessed a banana, because she knew Madison was growing bananas in her yard.

"Well, you guessed my favorite color—it's yellow. But, you are both wrong!" Madison giggled.
"I showed my class a kindness rock with a sunflower painted on it," Madison said.

"We painted kindness rocks last week with my cousins, Nora and Johnny.

My cousin Nora made a beautiful sunflower on one of the rocks."

Brenden looked at Billie with a strange look. "Why did you paint rocks, Billie? I've never heard of such a thing."

"To spread kindness! You paint a rock and turn it into a beautiful piece of art.

When a stranger finds the rock you painted, they will smile and be happy."

"That's really nice of you, Madison!"
renden exclaimed. "I'm going to ask my mom if we

can do that, because it sounds like fun."

Billie looked at house and saw her family waving from the window.   She smiled.

"Well, I know my family is really eager to hear about my first day of school.

Grandma and Grandpa even came over for dinner so they can hear all about it.

I'm glad you both had a great first day of school. It's very

different for all of us this year, but it sounds like we're each going to have a lot of fun."

"I think you're right, Billie." Brenden said. "We have plenty of new things to be excited about."

Madison nodded her head. "Alright, see you guys tomorrow!"

The friends all smiled as they walked back to their homes in their bubbles.

Tara Travieso is the author of *Billie and the Brilliant Bubble,* the first in the
Billie series released in June 2020. Tara was deeply moved by the positive
feedback she received from her first book. She wanted to continue the dialogue with
children and families about social distancing in *Billie Goes Back to School*.

Tara is the proud mother of two beautiful, young girls,
Alexandria and Addison, and is married to her college sweetheart, Robert.
They love to travel, enjoy good food, spend time outside, and
entertain family and friends.

After living in several exciting places around the world, including
New York, London, Washington, D.C., and Miami, Tara and Robert
decided to plant roots in their home state, Florida, for the next
chapter of their life. They now reside in Northeast Florida,
where they enjoy the lovely mix of seasons and the incredible beaches.

Shortly after their move, the COVID-19 pandemic struck. With schools
closed and business travel banned, Tara spent more time at home with her family.
She found the creative minds and wild imaginations of her children inspiring,
energizing, and increasingly important to maintaining happiness and balance.

CPSIA information can be obtained at www.ICGtesting.com
Printed in the USA
BVIW120518130920
588701BV00009BA/235